THE EXTREME ADVENTURES OF RECKLESS REX

THE BMX RACE: ADVENTURE ONE

Cindy Teddy Williams

Illustrated by Sarah Harris

WESTBOW®
PRESS
A DIVISION OF THOMAS NELSON
& ZONDERVAN

WestBow Press books may be ordered through booksellers or by contacting:

WestBow Press
A Division of Thomas Nelson & Zondervan
1663 Liberty Drive
Bloomington, IN 47403
www.westbowpress.com
1 (866) 928-1240

ISBN: 978-1-4908-8246-8 (sc)
ISBN: 978-1-4908-8247-5 (e)

Library of Congress Control Number: 2015908667

Print information available on the last page.

WestBow Press rev. date: 06/16/2015

Hey there! It's me, Rex. School's out for the summer, and I'm about to start my super rockin' summer adventure. I'm planning on becoming the next BMX Extreme racing all-star.

It all starts today on the first warm day of summer—you know, the kind of lazy summer day when you're finally completely free. Free from school, teachers, homework, and all the other generally annoying rules and requirements you had to deal with all year long. You're totally free—free to sleep in and free to spend time however you please because it's finally "your time." And I have plans, *big* plans for my summer—I will maximize the opportunity.

It seems like most kids in my neighborhood are always in need of some spending cash, and I happen to be one of those kids most in need of some extra funds. My best friend, Cruze, and I have some racing goals to accomplish. We're entering the end-of-summer BMX Extreme Showdown regional competition.

So on this first Saturday morning of summer, I'm doing some riding on my skateboard to round up as many lawn-mowing jobs as I can. I have a lawn mower that runs fairly well, and I figure it will last long enough to help me earn the amount of money I need to cover the entry fee and equipment expenses for the race.

My riding gear is pretty worn and ratty and in need of replacement; however, if I can't even come up with the competition entry fee, there will be no point in getting better riding gear. So I'm off, heading down the street with Blaze, my faithful dog and BFF. Instead of running, Blaze more like bounces by my side, circling and sniffing every scent that passes his way.

We noticed the old, run-down yellow house at the end of the street. At first glance one might think it was abandoned. "Hey, Blaze, let's go check it out; after all, the entire yard could sure use some mowing and cleaning up."

We started down the long, crooked sidewalk and approached the cracked steps leading up to the old, weathered door. I nervously clenched my fist and knocked on the door. At first, there was no answer. I knocked again. This time I thought I could hear slow, shuffling footsteps moving toward the door. Sort of reminded me of an old movie I saw from *Tales from the Crypt*—creepy!

The door slowly opened with a long, squeaky creak.

"May I help you?" said a deep voice.

"Ah, hey, mister. My name is Rex; I just live down the street and was wondering if you needed any help with your lawn maintenance this summer. I have a lawn mower, and I'd be willing to mow your lawn once a week." I could hear my voice quivering.

"Well," the old man answered, "I must agree it could use some extra care. I don't get around like I used to, and I guess the extra help would provide the neighbors with better scenery as well. I'm surprised I haven't been given a notice yet to clean things up. So how much are we talkin' for this mow job?"

"Well …" I carefully scanned the yard. "It looks like at least a twenty-dollars-a-week job, if that sounds fair to you."

"Sounds fair enough; I guess you got yourself some work."

"Hey, cool! How about I take care of it every Sunday morning?"

"Well … I'm usually in church on Sunday mornings. How does Sunday afternoon sound?"

"I think that'll work. I guess I'll have to practice at the track later on Sundays."

"Okay, Sunday afternoon it is. How 'bout two o'clock?"

"Sounds like a plan."

I blew out my loudest, piercing whistle, and Blaze came a-running.

"Hey, nice dog you got there—he's pretty smart."

"Yes, he is! Hey, by the way, I didn't catch your name."

"Albert … Albert Newton, but my friends call me Al."

"Okay, Mr. Newton. See ya on Sunday." I took off running down the old, cracked sidewalk to the street. "Sweet! I just got my first job of the summer."

I continued skating down the street, turning and weaving my skateboard as I contemplated just how many lawn jobs I would need to raise enough cash for the entry fee, equipment costs, and bike expenses for the upcoming BMX competition. Anyway, I was motivated now after landing my first job. At least one lawn was a start.

"C'mon, Blaze. Let's try to find some more work." Blaze wagged his tale and gave me an encouraging yelp, like he always does.

I managed to stop at eight or so more houses, with the hopes of getting at least two more jobs. After my last attempt, to no avail, I decided to call it a day. The quiet morning was giving way to the afternoon sun, and by now most people were running here and there, doing their Saturday errands, going to sports events, and tackling the usual weekend stuff.

I thought it was best to get home and take care of a few things before my mom returned from work. She had to put in extra time at work, and she'd added more household chores for my little sister and me to do. My mom did the best she could, but money was tight lately with her being the only support we had.

Later that afternoon I had plans to meet up with Cruze at the BMX track for some riding practice, which was a commitment I had to keep.

I swallowed the last bite of my sandwich as I arrived at the BMX track and looked around—no Cruze. "Where in the world is Cruze?" My eyes kept scanning the track. "I told him to be on time. We need to practice riding, and it's a perfect day. I guess I'll start without him," I muttered to Blaze. Blaze wagged his tail around like a spinning chopper. He loves to try to keep up with us as we ride around the track.

I rode my bike up the hill to the starting gate. "On your mark ... Three, two, one ..." I began to pedal as fast as I could, first hitting a left turn, then a right turn, and then taking the rhythm section at full speed. Next, I pulled off a tabletop jump and caught big air with a shaky landing. I continued around the berm turn, on over the double jumps, and finally across the finishing stretch of the course.

As I came to a stop, I heard a voice call out, "Pretty nice ride!" I looked over my shoulder and noticed Cruze.

"Hey, Cruze! 'Bout time you showed up—where've you been?"

"Oh, I just got a little tied up at home—sorry, dude. My mom is being a real house-cleaning warden lately. She wouldn't let me leave until I had all my chores done."

"Well, hurry and get over here! We need to get in a few more practice runs before dark."

"Definitely, let's do it!"

"The sun is starting to set behind the hills, Cruze."

"Yeah, it's getting harder to see the track. We probably should wrap it up for the day. What a great practice ride!"

"Hey, Cruze—look! Who's that coming over the hill?"

"I can't tell from here."

"Take a close look; doesn't it look like Duerott and that kid that got kicked out of school for selling drugs?"

"Yeah, I think you're right."

"We probably should get going. We don't need any trouble."

A voice echoed from the hill. "Hey, you guys!"

"Great, Cruze! That's all we need. They're trying to catch up to us. Let's just keep riding home."

"I don't know, Rex. Maybe we should just talk to 'em for a minute. Or else they'll think we're too chicken to talk to 'em. They'll think that's why we took off."

"I guess just a minute won't be a big deal—but whatever they say, don't trust 'em."

"Don't worry, I don't. I know what they're about."

"Hey, guys, what's up?" Duerott asked as he approached me and Cruze on our bikes.

"Not too much, Duerott. Rex and I are just out ridin'."

"Yeah, we just finished riding the track," I added.

"Cool, good day for riding. My friend Zach, here, and I have just been bumming around town," said Duerott smugly.

"Well, we've been spending most of our time riding at the track or trying to earn money for the BMX competition coming up," I replied.

"Wow! BMX competition, huh? Man alive, that sounds really serious." Duerott sounded like the usual sarcastic snake he was.

"Yeah, well, it *is* serious to us!" Cruze snapped back, his annoyance obvious.

"Well, if you run out of ways to earn money for this serious competition of yours, I just might be able to help you out with some funds," Duerott snidely replied.

"Yeah, so how you gonna help Rex and me do that, Duerott?"

"I have methods. Zach here and I have all kinds of funds. And like I said, we have as much time as we want to just bum around and do whatever we feel like," explained Duerott.

"C'mon, Cruze; we really need to get going."

"Yeah, I have to get home before dark too … Later, Duerott," Cruze said.

"Okay, see ya later," Duerott said. "You guys remember what I said now. If you're ever low on funds, I got you covered."

"He just thinks he's Joe Cool because he's older than us, Cruze," I said as we walked away.

"Yeah, he is a total jerk."

"C'mon, let's jump on our bikes and head for home; it looks like Blaze is already ahead of us."

"I'll call you later!" Cruze yelled as we hit the bottom of the hill and headed in different directions.

"Sounds good. See ya soon!"

The next morning was sleep-in Sunday—I love lazy Sunday mornings. I spent most of my time playing computer games and watching my little sister for my mom. As soon as my mom returned home from work, I was out the door to get down to Mr. Newton's house to mow his lawn.

"It's my first mowing job of the summer, and I can't be late."

In a rush I fumbled around with the rope while attaching my bike to the mower.

"That should do it. C'mon, Blaze, let's go get some work done."

I pedaled down the street and approached the old yellow house with Blaze at my side.

I jumped off my bike, untied the lawn mower, and with a couple of hard and fast pulls on the cord, I started the motor and began mowing Mr. Newton's lawn. As I crisscrossed my paths with precision, the lawn shaped up in no time. I was almost finished with the final lap around the yard when I heard Mr. Newton call out from his front porch.

"Hello there, Rex. The lawn looks great! I can't remember the last time it looked so clean and trimmed."

"Thanks," I yelled. "It really wasn't that bad once I got going."

"You look like you worked up a pretty good sweat. I just finished making some fresh, chilled iced tea. Come sit down, and I'll pour you a glass."

"Thanks, I could sure use that."

"I was running a little late from church today and wasn't sure if I would catch you before you finished the lawn. Glad I did," said Al.

"Actually, I was running a little late myself getting over here. I had to watch my little sister until my mom got home from work, but I made it. This is the best iced tea, by the way, even better than my mom makes."

"Glad you like it. Also, here is your payment for a job well done."

"Cool!" I stuffed the twenty-dollar bill into my pocket.

"So, Al, do you go to church every Sunday?"

"Well, just about every Sunday."

"Why do you have to go *every* Sunday?"

"I don't have to go. I choose to go," said Al.

"Why?" I asked, gulping down the last bit of my iced tea.

"Attending church helps me keep things in balance, like my priorities, and stay focused on what's really important in life," answered Al.

"So, what is really important in life?"

"Keeping the main thing the main thing pushes out all the less important details many folks get caught up with," explained Al.

"So just what *is* the main thing?"

"Serving God, the Creator of all things, and loving your neighbor as yourself … Helps the world be a better place," Al explained.

"You mean, like serving God and living the Golden Rule and all that stuff?"

"Pretty much!" Al replied.

"So you believe all that faith and church stuff is real?"

"Of course it's real! We all need to believe in something bigger than ourselves. If it's all about us, life can get pretty empty. We start getting sidetracked with all life's daily pressures and details until we lose our focus. Then life becomes empty and unfulfilling," Al explained.

"Hmm. So you're sayin' that if you keep the main thing the main thing, like God and the Golden Rule and stuff, then all the other things will just fall into place?"

"Life is full of ups and downs and can get downright turbulent at times, but with God in the center of it all, we have the assurance of a safe landing," answered Al.

"So that's why you go to church? To learn how to have safe landings?" I could feel my eyebrows rise with my question.

"That's partly why," answered Al.

"It doesn't seem like many people even care about the Golden Rule anymore. I mean, it seems like it just sounds like a good idea these days. I guess people don't believe it really works."

"Well, sometimes all we can do is just keep doing what's right, even if it seems like nobody cares. God always cares, and he sees what we do. He knows our hearts," Al answered.

"Sometimes I don't think he likes my heart or what's inside."

"That's exactly why many people keep running away from him. They think he is mad at them. Actually the opposite is true. If they understood just how much he loves them, they would accept his love and forgiveness. God wants to forgive. He's not mad at people," Al explained.

"Hmm. I've never thought of God being like that before. So you're saying that no matter what I've done, he would want to forgive me?"

"Yes, he would. All you gotta do is ask him."

"That's it? Just ask?"

"Yep, just ask," replied Al.

"I'll give that some serious thought. Thanks, Al."

"Anytime. If you ever have any more questions, you know where to find me."

"Yes, I do. I better get going for now though. Cruze and I are meeting at the track to practice some riding. I'll see you soon."

I hopped on my bike and headed for the track to meet Cruze.

As I approached the bike track, I noticed Cruze just ahead.

"Hey there, Cruze! So how's it going with coming up with the race money?"

"Not so good. I'm starting to run out of ideas to earn the money. I just wish there was a quick and easy way."

"Yeah, I hear ya. It's not exactly easy. Well, we better get a practice run in before it gets too dark."

"Great afternoon for a practice. I feel like things are coming together on my runs, especially the jumps."

"Yeah, me too," Cruze agreed.

"Well, we probably better be calling it quits for today. I'm supposed to be home before dinner."

"Sounds good. I'll see you tomorrow, Rex."

As we headed our separate directions for home, coasting down the hill, Cruze thought he heard someone calling his name.

As he glanced over his shoulder ... "Aw, man! Not him! Not Duerott. I don't need this right now," Cruze yelled out.

"Hey, hey, man! Just wait up a second; I just wanna ask you something."

"Well, what? Ask!"

"I just noticed you riding, and it came to my attention to check and see if you still needed any funds for anything. Business is really hoppin' for me right now, and I could sure use some help if you're interested."

"Interested in what, Duerott?"

"Just makin' a few product deliveries. I pay a real good commission."

"No thanks, Duerott. I know what you're about, and I'm not making any deals with you."

"Hey, I didn't say we're makin' any deals. I just offered you a quick, easy way to make some good cash by just makin' a few deliveries. That's all."

"What kind of deliveries?"

"Just product deliveries that I need delivered to some of my good customers. It's strictly business. Straight up."

"So, like, I would deliver the stuff to your customers?"

"Exactly. You are like my inside connection, so that would be worth paying you a good commission. Hey, just look at it like this—you're the inside track courier. You don't even know what's inside the packages. Just deliver the stuff and pick up your cash. It's that simple."

"Hmm. So you're sayin' I can't get in any trouble if I don't know what I'm delivering?"

"Exactly. Now you're hearin' me."

"Well, what would I have to do?"

"No problem. I'll meet you at the school bus stop tomorrow and give you all the details."

"All right, I guess. But I want to make it clear. I am *not* one of your customers."

"Relax, Cruze. I totally get it."

"I don't know why I still have a sick, queasy feeling in my stomach; it must just be your aura, Duerott. I don't trust you."

"Listen, man. After you see how much cash you're gonna earn for so little trouble, you'll start feeling better right away."

"Yeah, we'll see. I need to be getting home. It's getting late."

The next day was perfect weather for riding. I got an early start, jumped on my bike, and headed over to Cruze's house.

"Hey, Cruze! Hurry up and answer the door. We need to get some riding in while it's still early. We'll have the whole track to ourselves," I yelled as I continued to pound on the front door.

"Hold on. I'm comin' as fast as I can. Man, you're here early."

"I know. Hurry and get your bike; we can have the whole track to ourselves if we get there early."

"Okay, I'll grab my bike and meet you out front."

"Let's take the shortcut over the railroad tracks," I insisted.

"Sounds like a plan; so hey, Rex, I've been meaning to tell you. I found a way to get the money."

"How'd you do it so fast?" A minute went by, and Cruze didn't answer my question. "We'll, so how did you get the money?" I demanded.

"I … I just did one small favor for Duerott, just this once," Cruze said sheepishly.

"You *what*? Are you *crazy*? Have you completely lost your mind? Do you know what kind of trouble you would be in if you got caught? I can't believe you lowered yourself to his slimy, snake-level schemes."

"Well, time is running out, and I'm running out of options. I couldn't think of any other way to earn money," Cruze replied timidly.

I could hear the guilt in his voice.

"There are better ways," I said.

"So how are you doing on earning your funds, Rex?"

"Not so good either. I'm still working on it."

"So has it occurred to you that we're almost out of time?"

"Duh! Cruze, don't you think I know?"

"So then you understand why I did it. Unlike you, I don't even have a mowing job."

"Man, for your sake, Cruze, I sure hope nobody finds out you were involved with Duerott and his low-life schemes."

Another week of summer had already passed by. Why did summer vacation always seem to slip by so fast, especially when I needed more time? If it weren't for Al's lawn-mowing job, I wouldn't even have a chance to come up with the race fees. "C'mon, Blaze. I need to head over to Al's and take care of his lawn."

I waved at him. "Howdy, Al. I had some extra time today, so I thought I would get your lawn taken care of before the weekend."

"It's good to see you, Rex. How are things going with all the bike race plans?"

"Okay for me, I guess. I think I'll be able to have all the money in time."

"That's good news. So both you and Cruze will have done all the footwork to earn your way to the race, and the rest will be breaking records and making history."

"Well, I wish it was like that."

"I don't see why it can't be like that. You two have put in the work and practice, and now it's time to give it your best shot and reap the rewards."

"Yeah, I sure hope so."

CINDY TEDDY WILLIAMS

"What do you mean, you hope so? I thought this meant so much to you guys."

"It really does. I'm just worried about Cruze."

"What happened to him?"

"Well, nothing happened yet. It's what *could* happen that I'm worried about."

"What could possibly happen?"

"Cruze made a pretty bad choice. I promised I wouldn't tell anyone, but I know I can trust you, Al."

"For sure. Is there anything I can do to help?"

"I'm afraid not. The deed has already been done."

"Is Cruze in any danger?"

"Not yet, but he could be if the wrong people find out."

"Well, what do you need me to do?"

"I need to know what the right thing to do is. See, Cruze did a favor for a really bad guy in our neighborhood. This guy is a drug dealer, and everyone at school knows it. Cruze thought he wasn't going to be able to come up with the entry fees for the race in time. He told me he didn't see any other way to get the money. So he delivered some product to some other kids for this drug dealer."

"Hmm. I see. And the drug dealer paid him to make the delivery."

"Exactly!"

"Well, I definitely understand why you're concerned. That is a pretty risky thing to do. I'm sorry to hear he compromised so much."

"I know. Me too. I don't know what I am supposed to say or do. I mean, Cruze and I don't do any kind of drugs. We hate drugs! I feel like he let me down. We know everything about each other, and he knows how I feel about Duerott and the disgusting low-life person he is."

"Rex, I don't think Cruze meant to do any harm to your friendship. It sounds like he just felt desperate and chose the fastest, easiest way to get the money."

"I know, but it was still wrong."

"I agree. However, sometimes when people are under stress and pressure, they don't always make the best decisions."

"Yeah, he sure made a bad decision. More like a criminal decision."

"When the pressures of life seem to be closing in on us, we all are vulnerable to circumstances around us. Many times there is a way that seems right at the time, but in the end it leads to death and destruction. Remember, Rex, living in disloyalty to a higher moral code always leads to disharmony in life. Your conscience really is a good guide."

"I think I know and understand all that, but a lot of people, including me, sometimes just take the easy way out. I guess at the time it seems harmless, as long as you get what you want in the end."

"Unfortunately, many times that is true. But be assured that our choices always have consequences, and consequences are something we cannot choose. Cruze has made a choice, and now he has to possibly deal with the consequences of it."

"Yeah, you're right. So for now, all we can do is hope it turns out okay for him and he learns from his mistake. Thanks for listening, Al. I feel like I got a lot off my shoulders just telling someone."

"Anytime, Rex. I'm sure you'd do the same. Hey, I was just thinkin'. I could use some more help with a few additional jobs around my place, if you're interested. It's not the easy way out, but I pay a fair wage."

"Sure am interested! I need money fast; the race is in less than two weeks."

"Okay, you're hired. Be here at my house tomorrow morning at nine sharp."

"Sweet! I'll be here for sure. Thanks, Al! I need to get going for now. I'm supposed to meet Cruze for some riding practice. See you tomorrow!"

I better get down to the track. Cruze is probably wondering what's taking me so long.

"Hey there, Cruze! How is the track today?"

"It's pretty good. Hurry up and try it for yourself. I've already been here at least a half an hour."

"I know. Sorry. I was over at Al's house."

"So, Rex, have you got the money for the race yet?"

"No, but Al is helping me out by paying me to do some extra work around his house. He asked me to come over tomorrow morning."

"Is that the guy that hired you to mow his lawn?"

"Yeah, he's pretty cool. You should meet him."

"Yeah, maybe I will sometime. For now let's get some lap time clocked in."

"Okay, let's race each other. That way we can challenge each other to push ourselves."

"Ready, bikes on your mark ... Set! ... Go!"

We took off as fast as our feet would take us—down the hill and around the turns and through the course.

"Man, Cruze, you're gettin' fast. Your time has improved in a huge way. You stayed ahead of me the whole time!"

"Well, you were right on my tail the whole time, so I would say we are both pretty close."

We were completely out of breath and panting like a couple of race dogs.

"So, as I was sayin', we had a discussion. Al was telling me some things about right and wrong and good morals and things like that. It kinda started to make a lot of sense to me."

"So what is this guy? Some kind of do-gooder guru or something?"

"No man. He's really cool. He's a good guy."

"Cool. The world could sure use more good guys!" Cruse replied sarcastically.

"Whatever, Cruze! You haven't even met him."

"Well, like I said, maybe I will sometime."

"Well, my mom will be home soon. I'm supposed to be home before she is."

"Yeah, we better call it a day. That was a good practice run, Rex. Let's meet again tomorrow around four o'clock."

"Sounds like a plan. See you then."

By the time I got home, ate dinner, and lay down for what I thought would be a little while, it was already morning. I hurried and finished my chores, whistled for Blaze, jumped on my bike, and headed over to Al's house to earn some money. As I was turning into his driveway, I heard Al yell out. "Hello there, Rex. Top of the mornin' to ya!"

"Hey there, Al. Well, I'm here to work."

"Good to hear that, 'cause I got plenty. First of all, I thought this fence could use some brightening up, so you can get that white paint and brush on the porch and get started."

"Okay, I'll start with the outside first."

"I'm sure it will be a huge improvement when you've completed it, and the neighbors will appreciate it as well. While you get started, I'm going to go make us some lemonade."

"Thanks, Al. It won't take long 'til I work up a thirst."

Al walked across the lawn and over to the fence. "Looking better already, Rex. Here is some of my lemonade."

I gulped down a huge glassful. "Mmm, delicious!"

"Yes, it is. It was my mother's secret recipe. We've had it in the family for years."

"Well, it is very delicious. Definitely worth keeping around."

"So I was thinking about your friend, Cruze. I hope he didn't get into any trouble after dealing with that guy who sells drugs."

"Yeah, I know. I told him he was nuts to have any dealings with that guy. Everyone knows he's up to no good. So far we haven't heard of anyone getting caught or in trouble. I just hope he doesn't do it again."

"Me too. It would be such a loss for him to get in trouble so close to the day of your big BMX race."

"You're tellin' me! It's just less than two weeks away now."

"Well, Rex, the fence is looking great. Why don't you take a break? You can finish the rest tomorrow."

"Okay, I'll just finish up the front today. I need to meet up with Cruze again at the track soon anyway. C'mon, Blaze! We better head to the track; don't want to keep Cruze waiting. See you tomorrow, Al."

"It's another great day for riding. Hey, look over there, Blaze. Here comes Cruze."

"Hey, Rex. How are the jumps today?" Cruze yelled as he approached the track.

"Pretty smooth. Hurry and get over here and try 'em for yourself."

"Chill out, man. I'm going as fast as I can!"

"Man, I feel good. I think I'm as ready as ever. How 'bout you, Cruze?"

"Me too. I think all this practice is paying off."

"So we're down to less than two weeks until the race."

"Yep, and I'll be ready; my bike is running excellent, and I even had my mom sign all the entry papers already."

"So did your mom ask you how you came up with the money for the entry fees and equipment?"

"No, she didn't. Besides, I told her I would be getting some extra summer work."

"Well, I sure hope it all works out for you, Cruze. Dealing with Duerott gets a lot of people in trouble, and everybody knows he's always on probation."

"Don't worry about it. I have it all handled. I don't want to talk about it anymore!" Cruze snapped sharply.

"Okay, fine! But if something goes wrong, don't ever say you weren't warned."

"Don't worry. I won't!"

The next couple of weeks flew by like the wind. I continued doing jobs for Al and helping my mom look after my little sister. Cruze and I managed to meet every day at the track for riding practice.

It was finally the day before the big race. I was up before dawn; I could hardly sleep all night. I hopped on my bike and headed to Al's house. I just coasted in the driveway and heard Al call out from his garden. "Howdy, Rex! Tomorrow is the *big* day for you!"

"Yeah, I can hardly sit still. I barely slept last night. I'm already nervous; I just wish it was time to race already. I don't think I'll sleep at all tonight."

"Well, I believe you've done everything to prepare yourself. You've put in the time and effort. Just do your best and let God do the rest, and I'm sure you will come out on top."

"Thanks for your support, Al. Sometimes I'm not sure I'm good enough. I mean, some of the kids in the competition are amazing."

"Sometimes we all feel out of our comfort zone. But you'll never grow or improve if you don't put yourself to the test."

"I know, but I hate tests. I hate 'em in school, and I hate 'em in life."

"Life is full of tests, but once you get through the rough times and pass the tests, you will grow and be stronger next time."

"Man! So when are we ever done with tests? Don't we just get to relax when we get old and have it all figured out?"

"Well, Rex, life is a journey. Sorry, but nobody ever has it all figured out. We're constantly changing and growing. It takes a person a lifetime to be considered fully grown, and even then, we still don't know it all."

"I guess it was just wishful thinking to think I would have it all figured out someday."

"Don't forget we have the greatest hope. The hope of eternity! No more tests or trials and no more pain. Just an awesome eternity with the God who created us and loves us."

"Wow! Sounds nice. I'm sure I could be a champion BMX racer in heaven."

"I'm sure you could, Rex."

"I better get over to the track. Cruze and I are getting in one last practice before the race in the morning. If you don't have any plans, it would be really cool if you could come watch us, Al."

"I think I can probably make that happen. Meanwhile, my thoughts and prayers are with you and Cruze to have the best race ever!"

"I sure appreciate all you've done to help me out, Al. If it weren't for you hiring me to help around your house, I wouldn't even be racing tomorrow. But most of all, I want to thank you for being a good friend."

"Likewise, Rex. Let's just say I'm a proud sponsor and supporter of Rex, the regional BMX champ."

"Ha-ha! Now wouldn't that be a dream come true."

"Hey, dreams *do* happen. All things are possible with God on our side."

"Well, when you come tomorrow, can you make sure you bring God with you?"

"He'll be there."

"Okay, good, 'cause we'll need him. See you tomorrow, Al."

"See ya tomorrow, Rex."

The Race

The next morning came early. I was up before the sun. As I scurried around the house, making sure I had every last piece of equipment I could possibly need and inhaling my bowl of cereal, I decided it was time to head over to Cruze's house. He could probably use some help gathering his equipment; besides, it was better than wasting time and pacing back and forth around here.

"See ya later, Blaze. Sorry, buddy. No dogs allowed at the race." Blaze wagged his tail and yelped as if he understood. I hopped on my bike and rode down to Cruze's house.

I tried to knock softly to avoid waking up his entire family. No one answered, so I quietly opened the door and stepped inside. Cruze was coming down the stairs, carrying a full load of riding gear in his arms.

"Hey, dude! Let me help you with some of that."

"Wow, you're here early."

"Yeah, I couldn't sleep much at all last night. I've been up since dawn. I can't stop thinking about the race."

"I know how you feel, but hey, man, we're as ready as ever!"

"I sure hope so."

"In just a few hours we're going to be thrashing some bike track! I'll ask my mom if she can drop us off a little earlier at the track. We can have more time to size up our competition."

"Sounds like a plan."

We loaded our bikes. As we made the drive to the track, the closer we got, the more I began to feel a cold fear running through my body. I looked over at Cruze and noticed his foot tapping anxiously against the truck door. We could see the racetrack in the distance.

"Wow! Look at that racetrack, Cruze. It isn't exactly the neighborhood track."

"No, it sure isn't. It's totally awesome! I can't wait to get on it. This looks like a good place to unload our bikes."

"We better hurry and get checked in and get our competitor numbers."

"Maybe I can get my lucky number!" Cruze shouted.

"It's not about luck, Cruze. It's about skill."

"Well, I'll take all the help I can get—luck, skill, whatever. The line looks long already. Good thing we showed up early."

"C'mon; we better get checked in, Cruze."

As I glanced around at the crowd of racers, I heard a nagging voice in my head, asking, *Do you think you're good enough to go against all this top-notch competition?*

I tried to silence the voice by thinking positive thoughts. The negative, fearful voice, which was so loud and clear, kept overriding me. I began to feel that same old, cold fear running through my body again. In the back of my head, I remembered something Al had said. *If God be for me, who can be against me?*

I hung onto that thought as best as I could. It seemed to give me some peace.

"That wasn't too bad after all, Rex; I thought the line would move a lot slower. Hey, and guess what I actually got? One of my lucky numbers, number seventy-seven."

"That's good. Hope it brings you some luck. I got number eighty; I think that's a good number. Let's go check out the track before the race."

"Man, this track is huge, Rex. But I feel up for the challenge. I'm going for first place."

"Yeah, you and every other kid here."

"Hey, we're ready; we got just as good a chance as anyone else here."

"I think it's about time to head up the hill to the starting gate."

"May the race begin, and may one of us hold the title for the next regional BMX champion."

"Thanks for all your confidence, Cruze. I wish I had some of it. Seriously, I hope both of us do great."

"Okay, Rex, the time is *finally* here. I'll see you at the finish line, bro."

"Racers behind the gate!"

My ears rang as the sound of the announcer's voice blasted in the microphone. I began to feel the cold fear creeping up again. I noticed my hands were shaking as I gripped the handlebars. My knuckles were white as my grip increasingly tightened.

Cruze and I shot a last quick glance at each other as the announcer yelled, "On your mark!

Get set!"

Pop! The gun went off.

I felt a huge lump swell in my throat. As we took off, pedaling down the hill, I could feel my bike and body shaking like a jackhammer. I picked up speed as I approached the jumps. *Think, think. Think fast and stay low on the jumps*, I repeated to myself.

CINDY TEDDY WILLIAMS

I kept hearing the words: *Just finish. Just finish the race without crashing!* I managed to get one single thought in focus. *Look for an opportunity to attack and get ahead of the group.*

For a split second, the words Al had said popped in my head. *It's not about winning but how we finish the race that matters.*

Somehow those words filled me with a sudden burst of motivation.

I began pedaling faster.

I glanced over my shoulder and noticed that a couple of riders had already bailed off their bikes to avoid crashing.

At that point my thoughts returned to just finishing the race. *Even if I don't place, I can at least say I finished.*

My bike was still rattling like a can of nuts and bolts as I hit the bank turns and berms. Finally it appeared that I had overtaken the other riders. This fact motivated me even more as I could feel my heart pounding in my throat.

The rhythm section was coming up; I'd managed to muster up the speed and determination to keep going. I could barely see because of the salt stinging my eyes as my sweat poured off my head.

My bike was vibrating and shaking so much that I hoped it would just stay together to the finish. My arms and hands felt like rubber. I prayed I could just hold on a little longer.

Once again Al's words came to me. *God will be with you. He will give you strength for the race.*

"Oh, thank you, God!" I yelled out. "If you can hear me, please hear me now and help me finish this race!"

The last set of tabletop jumps were approaching. *If I get through these, I will be home free.* My feet pedaled as fast as I could move them.

I did a quick shoulder glance and noticed another rider down. He had a bright-orange shirt on, like Cruze's, but I couldn't get a clear look at him. All I could think was, *Finish, finish, finish the race.*

I managed to stay low over the triple jumps and not get too much air. My heart pounded in my head so loud I could barely hear myself think. All I could hear was, *God, please help me.*

I felt like I was on autopilot. My legs were just pumping with every ounce of energy I had left. I could hardly see the track in front of me; I just kept chanting, *Finish, finish, finish!*

I squinted through the stinging, salty sweat that filled my eyes and noticed the blurred red finish line ahead. I thought, *I'm gonna make it. Just a little farther.*

As I made the final push to cross the finish line, I heard the crowd cheering as I crossed over. I felt delirious but so relieved. I knew I had finished!

My whole body throbbed with pain, but it was a really good kind of pain. I managed to glance up in the stands and saw Al cheering and waving as he jumped up and down. At that moment I realized his friendship meant more to me than I'd ever understood before.

"Excellent race!" I heard Al yell as he ran to congratulate me.

"Thanks, Al." They were the only words I managed to speak while still trying to catch my breath. I reached out to shake his hand, and he pulled me into his chest, giving me the biggest bear hug I think I've ever had.

"You got third, Son! You got third place!" Al announced with pride to everyone around us.

"Yeah, I did! Not too bad for my first real race. And third place is good enough to stand on the podium and get a medal! Hey, by the way, where's Cruze? I haven't seen him since the start of the race."

"I haven't seen him either, and I'm afraid I have some bad news, Rex."

Al's eyes focused on the ground, gazing with disappointment.

I felt a lump swell in my throat, and a sick feeling festered in my stomach.

"What is it, Al? What happened?"

"I don't know exactly, but I do know Cruze didn't finish the race."

The sick feeling festering in my stomach suddenly grew into what felt like a tornado spiraling up my esophagus. I felt like I was about to lose what might be left of my breakfast.

What in the world was I supposed to say to Cruze when I saw him? I knew how much this race meant to him.

In the chaos of all the excitement and people crowding around, congratulating us, I momentarily glanced up and noticed Cruze in the distance across the track. He was limping along, pushing his bike toward the parking lot. He was walking slowly with his head hanging down.

In that second I felt like a knife had cut deep inside my heart and soul. I felt the most intense disappointment no words could describe. I looked over at Al and could tell he knew what I was feeling.

"What am I going to say to him, Al?"

"Probably best not to say anything. Just be a supportive friend, like you always are."

"Yeah, I think you're right. I'll just let him do all the talking."

"Well, for now you better get over to the podium and collect your medal and get some pictures taken."

"Sounds good. I hope I look good in the photos."

As I approached the podium and stepped up onto the third-place box, I scanned the cheering crowd. I couldn't hold in the pride I felt at that moment. A huge, wide grin was glued on my face; I couldn't stop smiling. I thought, *This is the coolest thing I have ever accomplished in my life.*

Looking around to wave at all the cheering fans wasn't too shabby either. My eyes began to see spots from all the camera flashes.

CINDY TEDDY WILLIAMS

Al was shooting photos along with all the other proud parents. I thought again, *I haven't even known him that long, and now I can't imagine him not being in my life.* I stepped off the podium after things seemed to have died down a little. I looked up, and suddenly there was Cruze, standing right in front of me.

"Excellent race, bro!" His hands reached out and grabbed my shoulders.

"Thanks, man."

It felt awkward for a bit as we walked in silence, heading toward the parking lot. I finally mustered up the courage to just ask the question.

"So, Cruze, what happened?"

"I don't even know; I was riding the course, and everything was smooth and fine. I hit the tabletop jumps, and the next thing I knew, my front wheel landed crooked, and I was out of control coming down the hill. I had no choice except to bail out."

"Oh, man! So that was you I noticed out of the corner of my eye when I landed the jumps. I glanced over and saw your orange shirt. Man, I'm so sorry, dude!"

"Hey, it ain't your fault. Stuff happens."

"You know that means you were ahead of me in the race, 'cause I didn't see you 'til after I landed the jumps."

"Don't remind me of the details. I'm sick to my stomach as it is."

"Sorry, I was just thinking you were in second place."

"I know. I don't know why that had to happen. I felt more ready than ever. I don't get it."

"Me either."

"Well, you placed in the top three. That's awesome."

"Next time we'll both be there."

"Yeah, I guess I do have a next time."

"Hey, look who's coming. This is the guy I've been wanting you to meet. Al, this is my best friend, Cruze. Cruze, this is my other best friend, Al."

"It's a pleasure to finally meet you, Cruze. I've heard a lot of fine things about you."

"Nice meeting you too, Al. Rex tells me you helped him out a whole lot with getting him into the race."

"Oh, he earned it all, and he was a great help to me just the same."

As we made our way to the truck to load our bikes, my thoughts were still in a whirlwind, swirling around in my head. One loud thought kept getting my attention, something Al had said to me. *Greater love has no one than this that he lay down his life for his friends.* I knew then that, without a doubt, Al was that kind of a friend.

The End

Moral: There is a way that appears to be right, but in the end it leads to death and destruction.

Our choices always have consequences.

CPSIA information can be obtained
at www.ICGtesting.com
Printed in the USA
BVHW031939040521
606452BV00005B/123